To Axier, Aner and Julen.
To my lovely family.

First published in 2015 by Child's Play (International) Ltd
Ashworth Road, Bridgemead, Swindon SN5 7YD UK

Published in USA by Child's Play Inc
250 Minot Avenue, Auburn, Maine 04210

Distributed in Australia by Child's Play Australia Pty Ltd
Unit 10/20 Narabang Way, Belrose, NSW 2085

Text and illustrations copyright © 2015 Zuriñe Aguirre
The moral right of the author/illustrator has been asserted

ISBN 978-1-84643-726-7
CLP100914CPL12147267

Printed in Shenzhen, China

1 3 5 7 9 10 8 6 4 2

A catalogue record of this book
is available from the British Library

www.childs-play.com

SARDINES of LOVE

by Zuriñe Aguirre

Once upon a time
there was
a grandfather
called Lolo.
He loved
eating sardines.

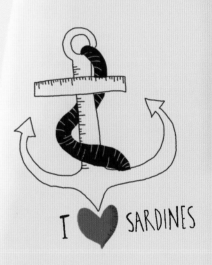

I ♥ SARDINES

He liked to eat them roasted
in the oven, or cooked on the grill.

He liked them fresh and he liked them in cans. He only ever left the bones.

He fished for sardines every single day.
Sometimes he fished with his rod,
near the lighthouse.

Other times he fished
for sardines from his boat
on the ocean.

Jeff the octopus
always came along.

Grandmother Lola sold sardines every day in her fish shop.

She hated sardines,
but she cooked them every
day for Grandfather Lolo.

One day, Lola sold all the sardines in the shop!

She didn't want Lolo
to go hungry.

So she took her rod
and went fishing.

Soon, she felt a tug.
A big sardine was pulling hard on the line.
Too hard!

Hard enough to send
Lola flying through the air,
straight into Jeff's mouth!

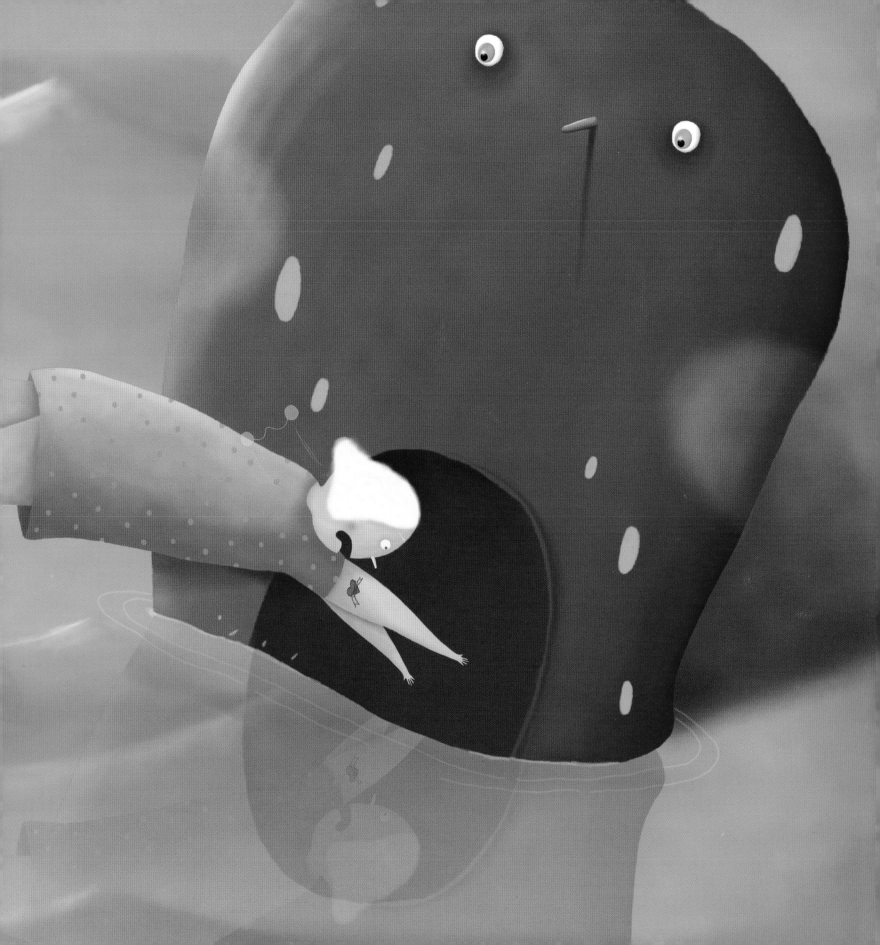

The hours passed. Lola began to feel hungry. But there were only sardines in Jeff's belly...

...lots and lots of sardines.

Back at home, Lolo was worried.
He did not know where Lola was.
He looked for her, and waited,
and looked again.

But Lola did not return.

Lola was getting really hungry,
She was so hungry she tried a sardine!

Then another, and another!
To her surprise, they were really tasty!

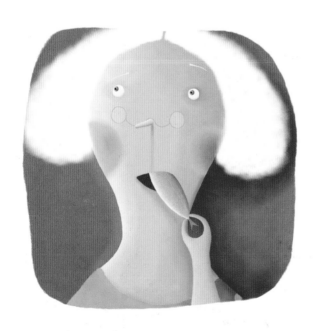 

Lolo was feeling very
sad without Lola.
He started to cry.

In Jeff's belly, Lola tried frying sardines. She made sardine jelly and she baked a sardine cake. She cooked sardine pizza and froze some sardine ice pops!

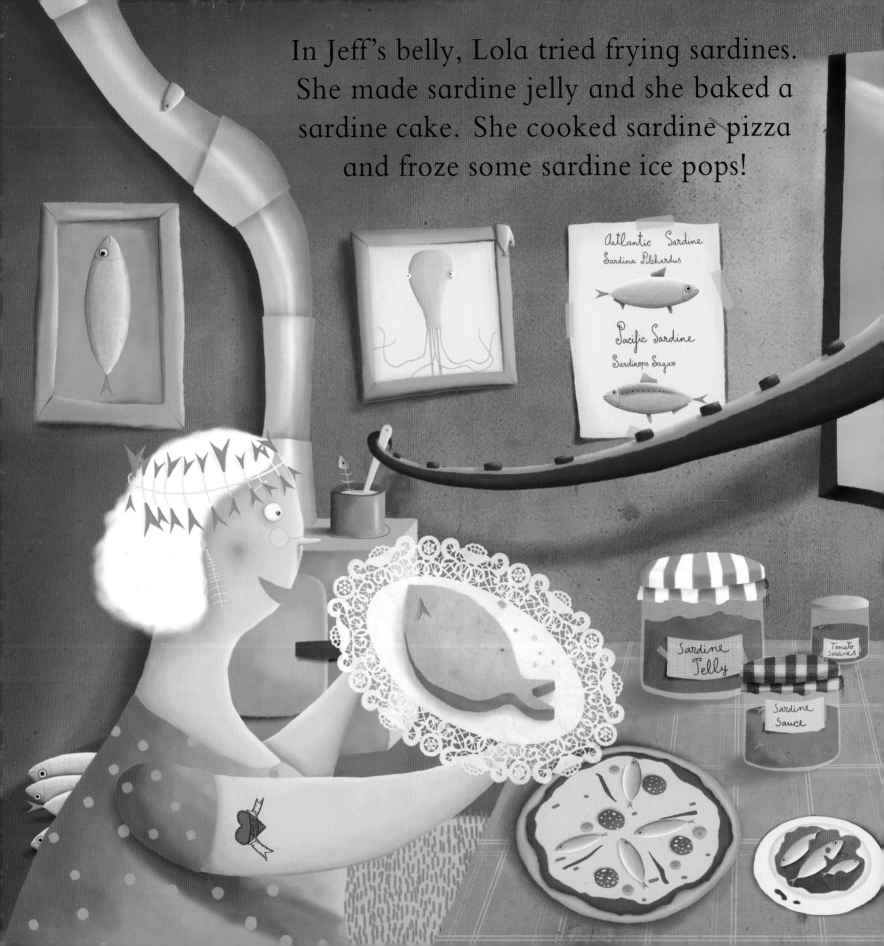

Meanwhile, Lolo could
not stop crying.

He cried so much, that he
began to float in his own tears!

He floated on his tears all the way to the ocean...

...and he found Lola again.

Now they were even happier than before.
They had all they ever needed –
LOVE and SARDINES!